# MAX FOUND
# TWO STICKS

To Andrea, who inspires me to hear life's music

—B.P.

# MAX FOUND
# TWO STICKS

## BRIAN PINKNEY

 HOUGHTON MIFFLIN    BOSTON • MORRIS PLAINS, NJ

California  •  Colorado  •  Georgia  •  Illinois  •  New Jersey  •  Texas

It was a day when Max didn't feel like talking to anyone. He just sat on his front steps and watched the clouds gather in the sky.

A strong breeze shook the tree in front of his house, and Max saw two heavy twigs fall to the ground.

4

"What are you gonna do with those sticks?"
Max's grandpa asked as he washed the front
windows.

Not saying a word, Max tapped on his thighs,
*Pat . . . pat-tat*.

6

*Putter-putter ... pat-tat.* His rhythm imitated the sound of the pigeons, startled into flight.

When Max's mother came home carrying new hats for his twin sisters, she asked, "What are you doing with Grandpa's cleaning bucket, Son?"

Max responded by patting the bucket, *Tap-tap-tap.*

*Tippy-tip . . . tat-tat*. He created the rhythm of
the light rain falling against the front windows.

After a while the clouds moved on and the sun appeared.
Cindy, Shaun and Jamal showed up drinking sodas.
"Hey, Max! Whatcha doin' with those hatboxes?"

Again Max didn't answer. He just played on the boxes,
*Dum . . . dum-de-dum.*

*Di-di-di-di. Dum-dum.*
Max drummed the beat of the tom-toms in a marching band.

"What are you up to with those soda
bottles?" his dad asked as he brought
out the garbage cans on his way to work.

Max answered on the bottles,
Dong . . . dang . . . dung.

*Ding . . . dong . . . ding!* His music joined the chiming of the bells in the church around the corner.

Soon the twins came out to show off their new hats.
"Hey, Max," they asked, "what are you doin' with those
garbage cans?"

Max hammered out a reply on the cans,
*Cling . . . clang . . . da-BANG!*

*A-cling-clang . . . DA-BANGGGG!*
Max pounded out the sound of the wheels thundering
down the tracks under the train on which his
father worked as a conductor.

Suddenly Max heard *Thump-di-di-thump . . .*
*THUMP-DI-DI-THUMP!* as a marching
band rounded the corner.

Max watched the drummers with amazement as they passed,
copying their rhythms. The last drummer saw Max.
Then with a nod and a wink, he tossed Max his spare
set of sticks.

"Thanks," called Max—and he didn't miss a beat.

The text for this book was set in 14 point Trump Mediaeval.
The illustrations were done on scratchboard with oil paint and gouache.

*Max Found Two Sticks*, by Brian Pinkney. Copyright © 1994 by Brian Pinkney.
Reprinted by arrangement with Simon & Schuster Books for Young Readers,
Simon & Schuster Children's Publishing Division All rights reserved.

Houghton Mifflin Edition, 2001

Printed in the U.S.A.

ISBN: 0-618-06200-9

123456789-B-06 05 04 03 02 01 00